Frida

¡Viva la vida!
Long Live Life!

By Carmen T. Bernier-Grand

Marshall Cavendish Children

TO THE STRONG WOMEN IN MY LIFE

Acknowledgments: So many people to thank: My daughter, Juliana Teresa Grand Kelly, let me steal her idea to write a book about Frida Kahlo; my editor, Margery Cuyler, showed confidence in me—again—even though I write in my second language; illustrator Carolyn Conahan and author Pamela Smith Hill began encouraging me as soon as they finished reading the first draft; my writing group pointed out unclear passages; Emily Hill corrected my German; my god-daughter, Rebecca Love, sent me information and two gorgeous books from the Frida exhibit at the Tate Museum; the work of my colleagues at Literary Arts' Writers in the Schools Program inspired me to write the recipe poem; librarian Julia Bergman at City College of San Francisco allowed me to read an old document on Frida and lured me to write a poem set in San Francisco; my sister, Lisette Bernier-McGowan, paid for my trip to Mexico; my husband, Jeremy Grand, took care of our demanding Maltese dog during my traveling; the attendants at the Frida Kahlo Museum and the Dolores Olmedo Museum answered my questions; the people of Mexico treated and protected me as if I were their child. To them and those whom I am forgetting: *¡Vivan largas vidas llenas de alegrías, salud y amor!* May you live long lives full of happiness, health, and love!

Marshall Cavendish Corporation, 99 White Plains Road, Tarrytown, NY 10591
www.marshallcavendish.us/kids

Library of Congress Cataloging-in-Publication Data
Bernier-Grand, Carmen T.
Frida : viva la vida = long live life / by Carmen T. Bernier-Grand. — 1st ed.
p. cm.
Summary: "Biographical poems about the life and work of Mexican artist Frida Kahlo"—provided by publisher.
Includes bibliographical references.
ISBN 978-0-7614-5336-9
1. Kahlo, Frida—Juvenile literature. 2. Kahlo, Frida—Poetry.
3. Painters—Mexico—Biography—Juvenile literature.
I. Title. II. Title: Long live life. III. Title: Viva la vida.
ND259.K33B47 2007
811'.54—dc22
2006014479

Photo research by Candlepants Incorporated

On the cover: **Self-portrait with Monkey (1938)**
Conger Goodyear commissioned this painting and said he would donate it to the New York Museum of Modern Art, where he was president, but instead he kept it until his death.

The text of this book is set in Tyfa.

Book design by Patrice Sheridan
Editor: Margery Cuyler

Printed in China
First edition
10 9 8 7 6 5 4 3 2 1

CONTENTS

Color photo with floral background © Nickolas Muray: Frida dressed in Tehuana clothing because she loved Mexico. The long skirt hid her short leg, and the colorful clothing accentuated her beauty.

MY BIRTH

My birth name is Magdalena Carmen Frida Kahlo y Calderón.
But I often say I am Frieda, German for "peace."

My birthday is July 6, 1907.
But I often say I was born in 1910,
daughter of the Mexican Revolution.

My birthplace is my grandmother's house in Coyoacán, Mexico.
But I often say I was born a block away,
in the U-shaped Blue House of my childhood,
a white building, until I painted it deep blue.

HUMMINGBIRD WINGS

I am a wounded hummingbird
caged in my room for nine months
with polio, crippling polio.

Warm towels soaked in walnut water
ease the pain in my leg,
a thin, drying twig.

I hide in the walnut wardrobe,
put on a white sock,
another on top,
and another.
Is the right leg as fat as the other?

The cage opens.
Now I have wings.

WILHELM (GUILLERMO) KAHLO

Frieda, lieber Frieda:
an acrobat on a bicycle;
roller skating, wrestling, climbing trees,
swimming, running, jumping over fences.
The son Herr Kahlo never had.

I call my German father "Herr Kahlo."
When he falls down,
his camera slung over his shoulder,
I make him breathe alcohol;
pull him to his feet
after his seizure ends.

I walk him to the river that flows
as slowly as the minutes of my life.
While he takes photographs to sell,
I collect thorny branches, shells, a handful of leaves.

At home,
I place the leaves under his microscope,
draw their milky white veins.

My Grandparents, My Parents, and I (1936): Standing on the patio of the Blue House, Frida holds a ribbon, her bloodline. Except for the baby, she painted her parents as they were in their wedding photograph. Her paternal, German grandparents are situated above the water; her maternal Indian grandfather and Spanish-Mexican grandmother are above the desert.

MATILDE CALDERÓN DE KAHLO

"*Mi jefe*" I secretly call *mamá*,
a Spanish-Mexican Indian
who never learned to read or write,
but she sure knows how to count money.

Mi jefe sent Herr Kahlo's daughters,
born to his first wife,
to live in a convent.
Luisita was seven, Margarita only three!

When chubby midget Cristina was born,
mi jefe replaced me with Cristina.
Mi jefe gave me away
to an Indian
who breastfed me.

Mi jefe shepherds us—
my older sisters, Matilde and Adriana,
my younger sister Cristina, and me—
every single day to Latin mass.

Mi jefe drowns the cellar mice
in a bucket.
She doesn't let go
until all are dead!

"Oh, *mamá*, you're so cruel!"

THE CACHUCHAS

Wearing a *cachucha* red-peaked cap
and blue overalls that hide my ugly leg,
I take the hour trolley ride from quiet Coyoacán
to the heartbeat of Mexico City.
"Cinco, cinco, cinco pesos," a vendor chants.
I buy a doll from him.

I run to *La prepa*,
meet the *Cachuchas*,
a gang of pranksters
who wear red-peaked caps like mine.
We read everything from Dumas to Azuela;
ride a donkey
in the corridors to protest
classes that bore us.

None of this is enough for me.
I want to move to San Francisco,
City of the World!

Frida at 19 (1926): Frida always tried to hide her shattered leg. In this photo—taken on February 7, 1926 by her father Guillermo Kahlo—she hides it with her left leg. Her house was decorated with Persian rugs and French furniture. Frida was an avid reader.

Portrait of Diego Rivera (1937): Frida often called Diego "Frog-face."

DIEGO

I soap the stairs
to the amphitheater stage,
hoping to see *panzón* slip and fall.

Diego points his feet out.
Like a puppet on strings,
that fat-bellied frog climbs each step.

I am hiding behind a huge pillar,
watching him paint a mural
as big as the stage.

His blonde model, Nahui, poses.
"Watch out, Diego!"
I scare him with a lie. "Here comes Lupe!"

Diego's ex-wife, Lupe, arrives
after Nahui is gone.
"Watch out, Diego! Here comes Nahui!"

THE ACCIDENT

If only I hadn't lost my little toy parasol!

I jump off a running bus to find it.
No luck. I buy a *balero*, a cup-and-ball toy.
 jump onto a brightly painted bus,
sit in back on a bench along the side
near a painter with a toolbox
that holds powdered gold paint.

In front of the San Juan market,
a trolley car plows into our bus!
I bounce forward.

The bus bends, bends, bends.
Hits a wall.
Bursts into pieces!

The *balero* is jolted from my hand.
Where does it go?
A handrail
P
I
E
R
C
E
S
my hipbone.

Powdered gold sprinkles
on my blood-drenched body,
a glittering red tutu.
"¡La bailarina!" a child yells.
"Please, help the ballerina!"

A man carries me to a pool table,
pulls out the handrail.
¡AYYYY!
The ambulance sirens sound mute under my cries.

If only I hadn't lost my little toy parasol.

The Bus (1929): Frida's 1925 accident took place on a similar bus.

Life Begins Tomorrow

Enclosed in a cast,
it hurts a lot to laugh with *carcajadas*.
Spinal column broken in two places,
pelvis in three,
ribs in two,
right leg in seven,
left elbow dislocated,
deep abdominal wounds.
But I laugh with *carcajadas*,
for Death didn't take me.
"I'm still alive," I tell *mi jefe*.
"And besides, I have something to live for.
That something is painting."

Recipe for Self-Portrait

7 Herr Kahlo's oil paints
1 large pain
1 liter of tears
Look at self, black hair silk girl,
in the daily mirror
on the underside of my bed canopy.
Draw self, the subject I know best.
Squeeze oil paints on a heart-shaped palette:
    Green: Warm and good light.
    Reddish purple: Aztec. Old blood of prickly pear.
    Brown: Color of mole.
    Yellow: Madness, sickness, fear.
    Black: Nothing is black. Really nothing.
    Cobalt blue: Electricity and purity. Love.
    Magenta: Blood? Well, who knows?
Slay pain, saying what I can't say otherwise.
Drop slain pain in an earthenware tureen.
Pour in tears.
Soak pain in tears until completely dissolved.
Dab brush in tear solution.
Dip brush in oil paint.
Respect the brush's wishes.
Let portrait dry for 2 to 4 days.
In the meantime, sing *La Malagueña*.

"You Have Talent"

Should I keep painting now that I have healed?
Mi jefe and Herr Kahlo can't afford more X-rays.
To pay for my medical bills,
they mortgaged the house,
auctioned off the French furniture.

I hide my ugly leg and plaster corset
beneath a Tehuana outfit with blossoming ruffles of lace.
Swaying my skirt as the wind sways a flower,
I go to show Diego Rivera my self-portrait.

"Diego, come down!" I call out.
And he obeys!
"Look," I say, "I have not come here to flirt.
I have come to show you my painting.
If you are interested in it, tell me; if not, likewise,
so I will go to work at something else to help my parents."

"I am very interested,"
Diego says as if he were my father.
"Go home, paint a painting, and next Sunday
I will come and I will tell you what I think."

On Sunday
I put on overalls, like Diego's,
and climb a flowering orange tree.
When he arrives, I whistle
The Internationale, a socialist song.

His bulging eyes look up at me
as no human eyes have looked at me.
I laugh, climb down—
my hand nesting in his soft hand.
I usher him inside,
show him three portraits.

"You have talent!" he says.

Portrait of Alicia Galant (1927): Alicia Galant became Frida's friend in 1924 at the National Preparatory School. Frida painted this at about the time she started showing Diego her work.

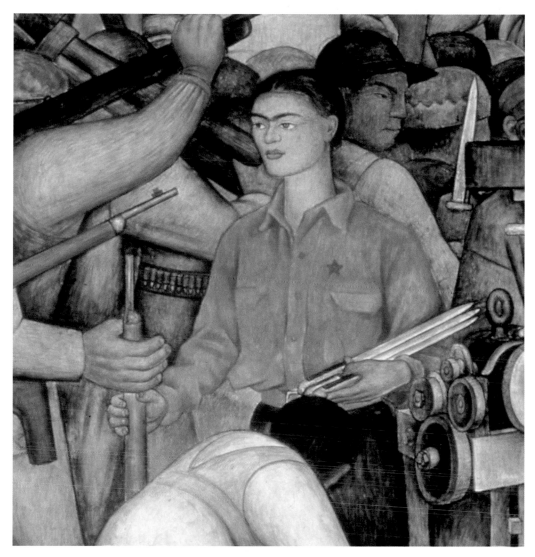

Detail from *Insurrection* (1928): Frida distributes arms in Diego Rivera's mural at the Ministry of Public Education in Mexico City.

Frida and Diego Rivera (1930-1931): A wedding portrait completed two years after their marriage. The inscription on the ribbon the dove is carrying says: "Here you see us, me Frieda Kahlo, with my beloved husband Diego Rivera. I painted these portraits in the beautiful city of San Francisco, California, for our friend Mr. Albert Bender, and it was in the month of April of the year 1931."

¡EXTRA!

Wednesday, August 21, 1929

Coyoacán—Today the marriage
between an elephant and a dove
took place in a civil ceremony
in the ancient hall.
The twenty-two-year-old bride
Frida Kahlo wore
a Tehuana peasant dress
and a *rebozo* created by the people
for the people
who belong to the people.
The forty-three-year-old,
bulky groom Diego Rivera,
sported a peacock feather
in his Stetson hat,
a wide leather belt,
huge miner's shoes,
and paint-stained pants
that looked as if he had slept in them
for a week.

Self-portrait on the Border between Mexico and the United States (1932): The inscription on the stone says: "Carmen Rivera painted her portrait in 1932." The press called her Carmen Rivera and referred to her as "the petite wife of Diego Rivera who sometimes dabbled in paint."

SAN FRANCISCO

Women in slinky dresses and pert little hats
stare at my frilly skirts, my sun-shaped earrings,
the ribbons of purple light adorning my braided hair,
the thousand-year-old jade necklace Diego gave me.
I giggle, enjoying the attention!

Diego disappears for days,
painting a mural at the San Francisco Stock Exchange,
another at the California School of Fine Arts.

I hardly paint.
Instead I play at being *his* wife.
Frida Kahlo *de* Rivera
—"*de*" Rivera, "of" Rivera—
I belong to my owner.

Mother and Child

To nourish the four-month baby in my womb
I drink two glasses of cream.
It comes back up!
Was *mi jefe* as sick when I was in her womb?

Mi jefe. Matilde Calderón.
Dark-skinned Tinker Bell from Oaxaca.
Was *mi jefe* as lonely during her pregnancies
when Herr Kahlo hid in his room—absent, like Diego?

Diego finds me in a pool of blood.
An ambulance rushes me
to the hospital in Detroit.
When doctors roll me down a corridor,
I point at the ceiling's colorful pipes.
"Look, Diego! How beautiful!"

On July 4, 1932, as slowly as a snail,
I lose my baby.
On September 15, *mi jefe* dies.

I paint
     and paint
          and paint
               all my pain.

Manhattan

Manhattan: Center of poverty
—the poverty of having everything,
the poverty of having nothing—
Bread lines, crowds of demonstrators.

My dress hangs empty.
I don't want to be here.
It is terrifying to see the rich
having parties day and night
while thousands and thousands of people
are dying of hunger.

My Dress Hangs There (1933): Frida pokes fun at American values.

Portrait of Cristina Kahlo (1928): Frida and Cristina later reconciled and remained companions until Frida's death.

DOUBLE DISGRACE

Why does this affair hurt more than the others?
She was my sister whom I loved the most.
Diego and Cristina—a double disgrace!
It is all about him. Her. Them. Me.
It is going to take me years to get out
of this mess I have in my head.
Why did Cristina steal him from me
when she has everything I do not?
Two good legs, green eyes, two children!
Cristina's husband had left her,
and Diego offered her his tenderness.
It would be easier to forgive Cristina
than to forgive Diego.
Diego blames the affair on me
for making him return to Mexico.
I suffered two grave accidents in my life.
One the streetcar,
the other Diego.

MY DIEGO MY CHILD

Diego is crossing the bridge
between his large, dark-pink studio
and my small, sky-blue studio.
He knocks on the glass door dividing us.
He pleads with me to open it.

I shift my focus
to my unfinished self-portrait,
then to the mirror, and talk to myself.
Why do I call him *my* Diego?
He never was and will never be.

Time waits.
Is he still there?
He's such a child in overalls,
his shoes stomping across the bridge.
He scurries down the spiral
staircase to our front patio,
strides by the organ cactus fence.

A knock on my downstairs door.
It's him. I stay still.

Diego my child Diego my lover Diego my husband.
(Diego never has been and never will be anyone's husband.)
Diego my mother Diego my father Diego my son.

My paintbrush drops.
He has climbed three flights of spiral stairs.
He's crossing the bridge.
He's huffing. He's sweaty. He's puffing.
He pleads forgiveness, full of shame.
I slide open the thin glass door.
Rivers of sweat mix with tears.

The Love Embrace, the Earth (Mexico), Diego, Me, and Señor Xolotl (1949): Here Frida is
Mother Earth and Diego's mother. Frida's hairless dog, Señor Xolotl, rests by her feet.

Self-Portrait with Cropped Hair

Frida Kahlo, a divorced woman—
I move
my parrots, hairless dogs,
deer, spider monkeys, and toys
to the U-shaped house of my childhood.
I paint the outside deep blue
to keep the evil spirits away.
Instead of my family's Persian rugs, I have *petates*.
Instead of the French sofa, Mexican chairs.

Why did Diego ask me for a divorce?
Was he having another affair?
Or did he learn about mine?

Men are kings. They direct the world.

I put on Diego's suit
(it smells like him).
I sit in a Mexican yellow chair
and chop off my hair—
the hair he adored.
I look like a man,
but I leave my earrings on.

Self-portrait with Cropped Hair (1940): The words of the song say: "Look if I loved you, it was for your hair. Now that you are bald, I don't love you anymore."

HEADLINES

I don't know what they see in my work.
Why do they want me to have a show?

New York has painter Frida Kahlo's first solo show.
Actor Edward G. Robinson buys four of Frida Kahlo's paintings.
Frida Kahlo receives Mexican prize for *Moses*.
Frida Kahlo exhibits her art in Mexico and Paris.
Paris designer launches a line of Frida Kahlo's fashion.
Pablo Picasso gives Frida Kahlo earrings shaped like hands.
Picasso says he is not capable of painting a head like those of Frida Kahlo.
The Louvre buys Frida Kahlo's *The Frame*.

For that price they could buy something better.

The Frame (1938): The Louvre bought this self-portrait in which Frida framed her face with birds and flowers painted on glass.

Second Marriage

"Give your Cupid back his foundation,"
Diego writes from San Francisco.

What he's asking me to do is as difficult
as having to gather the strands of hair
I chopped off last year
and weave them into a braid.
Our marriage would never be perfect—
unruly hairs would stick out of such a braid.

On December 8, 1940, in San Francisco,
Diego and I marry for the second time.
But like the strong women of the Isthmus of Tehuantepec—
who run the market, handle the money, and rule their men—
I provide for myself selling my art.

Before, he was the father and I was the child.
Now I am the mother, he is the child.

Self-portrait with Braid (1941): Frida wears a necklace that Diego probably gave her. The leaves seem to be ready to attack her, indicating that she may still feel consumed by Diego's infidelities.

"What Do I Live For?"

Will I ever heal after thirty-one surgeries:
hip, spine, foot. And twenty-eight corsets:
three made of steel, three of leather, the rest of plaster?

"What do I live for?" I ask Diego. "For what purpose?"
He has rented a hospital room to be near me.
"So that I live, *Fisita!*" he answers. "So that I live."

Nothing is equal to the green-gold of his eyes.
Nothing compares with his hands.

"My darling child," I ask him,
"do you want a little piece of fruit?"
"*Chi,*" he answers instead of "*sí.*"

The next bout of pain, I take *a la mexicana*,
suffering but not protesting.
Diego grabs a tambourine,
dances like a bear,
makes my eyes twinkle.
He embraces me,
rocks me to sleep.
My Diego, I'm no longer alone.
You lull me to sleep and make me come alive.

Tree of Hope, Stand Firm (1946): The sunny side of the painting shows Frida anesthesized in a hospital trolley with her back incisions bleeding. The moon side shows Frida crying yet dressed in red. Determined to fight for her life, she is wearing a pink corset and holding another as if it were a trophy. The banner that says "Tree of hope, stand firm" comes from a Veracruz song that, ironically, continues with the words: "Don't let your eyes cry when I say goodbye." The banner's pole looks like a paintbrush that has been dipped in red paint or blood.

Wounded Deer

My barren landscapes show my barren self.
I have lost three children.

Four arrows in my heart
to remind Diego how his shots have made me bleed.

Shooting pains in my hip,
Shooting pains in my foot,
Shooting pains in my spine.

I am not sick.
I am broken.
But I am happy to be alive.

The Little Deer (1946): Frida's pet fawn, Granizo, may have been the model for this painting. The word CARMA in the lower left suggests that the bad luck in Frida's life came from cosmic forces, not because of anything she did.

LOLA'S GALLERY

In my homeland of Mexico
my solo art show is tonight.
My canopy bed is displayed.
My paintings on the walls have light.

At eight, strangers, friends, family
pour into Lola's gallery.
They linger, looking at my art,
paintings of my life's misery.

Blue House monkeys and bald dogs,
the wounded deer in dead woodlands,
Diego's forehead eye of wisdom,
my earrings in the shape of hands.

My motto: Tree of Hope, keep firm!
Steel corset, Tehuana laces,
broken column, baby doll bed,
fruit alive and thorny necklaces.

"No artist in Mexico can
compare with her!" Diego cheers.
"Is she coming?" visitors ask.
"Or is she too sick to be here?"

Sirens blare! Everybody rushes
to see me, what's left of Frida,
carried in and put on my bed.
"Long live life! *¡Viva la vida!*"

"Thanks to myself and to my will
to live among those who love me.
And for all those I love: Long live
joy, life, and Diego, who loves me!"

Self-portrait as a Tehuana (Diego in my Thoughts), 1943: Frida, wearing her most favorite costume from the Isthmus of Tehuanatepec, had Diego constantly in her thoughts. She began this painting in August 1940, the year they divorced. She wore ruffles and laces, hoping to win Diego back. The roots coming out of the flowers look like strands of spider webs reaching out to trap him

Portrait of Natasha Gelman (1943): Natasha Gelman and her husband, Jacques, bought a number of paintings by Diego and Frida.

Self-portrait Dedicated to Leon Trotsky (1937): On his birthday, Frida gave this portrait to the exiled Soviet revolutionary, Leon Trotsky, with whom she had an affair. The letter says: "To Leon Trotsky with all affection I dedicate this painting on November 7, 1937. Frida Kahlo. In San Angel, Mexico."

The Chick (1945): Frida's pet hen laid an egg and then died. Using a lamp, Frida warmed up the egg and a chick was born. In this painting big bugs threaten the orphaned chick. By 1945 both of Frida's parents had died and she had marital and health problems that seemed bigger than life.

Wings to Fly

There is only one, and I want two.
For me to have two they must cut one off.

The Mexican poor know
how to silence pain with alcoholic *pulque*.
I raise the bottle, toast to my solitude,
drink it like a *mariachi*.

Everything is upside down:
Sun, feet, me, moon—
cigarette after cigarette.
You are killing yourself!

I drink to drown my pain,
but the damned pain learns to swim.
A shot of the painkiller Demerol—
Sleep Sleep
Sleep Sleep
Sleep
Sleep
I'm falling asleep.

But I have to paint!
I have to paint before the pain returns.
Poppy red paint smudges my hands.
Poppy red paint stains my clothes.
I have to paint before there is only one footprint.

Feet, what do I need them for
if I have wings to fly?

Without Hope (1945): Doctors made Frida eat pureed food every two hours.

Viva la vida (1954): Eight days before her death, Frida added the finishing touches to her last painting.

¡Viva la Vida!
Long Live Life!

Wearing the white *huipil* with the lavender tassel,
hiding my amputated leg in red-leather boots,
I wheel the wheelchair to the Blue House studio
that Diego so lovingly built for me.

I dip the brush in blood-red paint
and, embracing life with all its light,
I print on a watermelon cut open—like I am—
 ¡Viva la vida!—
a hymn to nature and life.

In my red-leather diary,
I draw the silent Angel of Death.
I hope the exit is joyful.
And I hope never to come back.

I curl up, a snail in bed.
Diego cuddles and caresses me,
the air caressing the earth.
"I was shattered and you restored me."
I slip an antique peacock ring on his finger .
"I feel I am going to leave you very soon."

No me olvides

Frida Kahlo dies on July 13, 1954,
a day of heavy gray skies in Coyoacán,
her braided head resting
on an embroidered pillowcase that says:
No me olvides, amor mío.
Don't forget me, my love.
Diego looks as if his soul has been cut in two:
"Too late now I realized
that the most wonderful part of my life
had been my love for Frida."
Life goes by, and sets paths,
which are not traveled in vain.

From the Letters and Diary of Frida Kahlo

"Only a mountain knows the core of another mountain."

"There is nothing more precious than laughter. It is strength to laugh and lose oneself."

"I never feel disappointed in life."

"I have never expected anything from my work but the satisfaction I could get from it by the very fact of painting and saying what I couldn't say otherwise."

"The most important thing for everyone in Gringolandia is to have ambition and become 'somebody,' and frankly, I don't have the least ambition to become anybody."

"The reason why people need to make up or imagine heroes and gods is pure fear . . . fear of life and fear of death."

"Nothing is absolute. Everything changes, everything moves, everything revolves, everything flies and goes away."

"Nobody is separate from anybody else. Nobody fights for himself. Everything is all and one."

Frida Kahlo:
1907-1954 and Beyond

During her lifetime, Frida Kahlo produced more than 138 paintings, many of which were disturbing self-portraits reflecting her turbulent life.

Born on July 6, 1907, in Coyoacán, Mexico, she was one of four daughters of a Jewish Hungarian-German father and a Spanish-Mexican Indian mother. When Frida was six, she suffered from polio. It left her with a shriveled right leg and a slight limp.

Although Frida doodled in her school notebooks, drew on letters to friends, and twice tried to finish a self-portrait, she did not think of herself as an artist. She wanted to become a doctor. In 1922 she entered the National Preparatory School's pre-medical program.

She had to abandon her studies when on September 17, 1925, she was in a bus accident that left her with a shattered pelvis and fractures in her right leg, back, and collarbone. For the rest of her life, she suffered from the injury and had thirty-one operations.

During her recuperation from the bus accident, Frida began to paint. Three years later she showed her work to muralist Diego Rivera, who encouraged her to keep on painting. He thought she was a better painter than he.

Despite their difference in age, on August 21, 1929, they were married. They had a stormy relationship full of infidelities, miscarriages, divorce, remarriage, and Frida's constant health problems.

Frida painted herself because she was often bedridden and could see her reflection in a mirror attached to her bed's wooden canopy. She painted her physical and emotional pain. But when not confined because of illness, she enjoyed life—laughing, dancing, and singing among her friends, family, and with Diego.

Frida and Diego were members of the Mexican Communist Party (PCM). Yet they were more socialists than communists. In 1929 the PMC expelled Diego because of ideological differences. Frida, in support of her husband, resigned her membership.

Her feelings for Diego changed when in 1934 Diego had an affair with Frida's younger sister Cristina. In retaliation, Frida had a brief affair with the exiled Soviet revolutionary, Leon Trotsky, whom Diego had brought to Mexico.

Diego and Frida had hurt each other too much. They divorced.

While Diego continued his affair with Cristina for a year, Frida had romantic relationships with men and women. She also traveled and tried to become economically independent by selling her paintings. Her first solo show that had been held at Levy Gallery in New York in 1938 was followed by many other successful exhibits in the United States, Europe, and Mexico.

Despite their turbulent history, Frida and Diego always loved one another. In 1940, a year after their divorce, they remarried. From then on, Frida treated her husband like the child she never had, and he enjoyed it.

On July 13, 1954, two years after the amputation of her shriveled leg, Frida Kahlo died at age forty-seven. While experiencing extreme pain, she asked Diego and Cristina to help her die. It is possible they did, but no one will ever know. Death records indicate Frida died of a pulmonary embolism, and no autopsy was performed.

Frida's ashes rest in a pre-Columbian urn in her childhood home, the Blue House in Coyoacán, which became the Frida Kahlo Museum. But she—who loved life and continually used the phrase "Please don't forget me!"—lives on in her letters, diary, Blue House, and paintings.

CHRONOLOGY

1907—On July 6, at 8:30 AM, Magdalena Carmen Frida Kahlo y Calderón is born in Coyoacán, Mexico.

1910—On November 20, the Mexican Revolution begins. Frida claims she was born with the revolution in 1910.

1913—Frida contracts polio.

1922—Frida enters the National Preparatory School where she's a member of the *Cachuchas* and teases muralist Diego Rivera as he paints his mural, *The Creation*.

1925—On September 17, Frida is badly injured in a bus accident.

1927—Frida goes through three plaster corsets.

1928—Frida becomes a member of the Mexican Communist Party. She shows her paintings to Diego Rivera.

1929—On August 21, Frida and Diego get married in Mexico City. Diego is expelled from the Mexican Communist Party (PCM). Frida resigns from the PCM.

1930—At the beginning of the year, Frida's first pregnancy is terminated because the fetus is not in position. On November 10, Diego and Frida arrive in San Francisco, where he has a commission to paint the Stock Exchange mural.

1931—Frida's painting, *Frieda and Diego Rivera*, is shown in San Francisco. Frida and Diego return to Mexico briefly before going to New York City for Rivera's solo exhibition at the Museum of Modern Art.

1932—On April 21, they move to Detroit where Diego has been commissioned to paint the *Detroit Industry* mural. On July 4, Frida has a miscarriage at the Henry Ford Hospital. On September 15, her mother dies.

1933—In March the couple moves to New York City where Diego begins a mural in the Rockefeller Center that gets cancelled when he paints the communist leader Lenin. On December 20, Frida and Diego move to their twin apartment-studios in San Angel, Mexico City. Diego and Frida's younger sister Cristina have an affair that lasts a year.

1934—Frida's third pregnancy is terminated. She undergoes an appendectomy and has an operation on her right foot in which two toes are removed. Frida briefly visits New York with friends.

1935—Frida and Diego temporarily separate, and Frida moves into an apartment in Mexico City. They later reunite in San Angel.

1936—On April 29, Frida has a third operation on her foot.

1937—The exiled Soviet revolutionary, Leon Trotsky, and his wife, Natalia, arrive in Mexico. Frida has an affair with Trotsky. Four of Frida's paintings are included in a group exhibition in Mexico.

1938—November 1 to 15, Frida has her first solo show in Julian Levy's gallery in New York City. She sells four paintings for two hundred dollars each to actor Edward G. Robinson. She has a fourth operation on her foot.

1939—In March, Frida travels to Paris to exhibit her work in the Renou & Colle gallery. The Louvre purchases *The Frame*. She moves to the Blue House, her childhood home in Coyoacán. She helps refugees from Fascist Spain reach Mexico. She suffers from a fungal infection on her right hand and has severe spine pain. On November 6, Frida and Diego divorce at his request.

1940—In January, *The Two Fridas* and *The Wounded Table* are exhibited in the International Surrealism Exhibition in Mexico. She also exhibits her work in San Francisco and New York. In September she travels to San Francisco for treatment from Dr. Leo Eloesser. She has a severe kidney infection and anemia. On December 8, she and Diego remarry in San Francisco.

1941—On April 14, her father dies of a heart attack. Diego moves to the Blue House. Frida's art is exhibited in Boston.

1942—Frida's art is shown in two New York City exhibitions.

1943—In January, Frida's work is included in "Exhibition of 31 Women" in New York City. Frida teaches at the Ministry of Public Education's School of Painting and Sculpture, known as *La Esmeralda*. Poor health prevents her from traveling to Mexico City. She teaches six of her students at the Blue House. They call themselves *Los Fridos*.

1944—Frida undergoes spinal taps, wears her first steel corset, and her fourth pregnancy is terminated.

1946—Frida receives second prize from the Ministry of Public Education for her painting *Moses*. She goes to New York and has surgery in which a metal bar is attached to her spine. Large doses of morphine are prescribed for her.

1950—Frida undergoes a total of seven spine operations and spends nine months in the Hospital Inglés in Mexico City. Diego rents a hospital room to be near her.

1951—Frida spends most of the day in a wheelchair, taking a number of painkillers.

1952—Frida attends her first solo show in Mexico at Lola Alvarez Bravo's gallery.

1953—Frida is documented as a member of the Mexican Communist Party. In August, her gangrened leg gets amputated below the knee.

1954—Diego is permitted to rejoin the Mexican Communist Party. On July 2, Frida has pneumonia but joins Diego in a demonstration to protest the United States's intervention in Guatemala. On July 13, Frida dies in the Blue House in Coyoacán, Mexico.

1957—On November 24, Diego dies of heart failure in his San Angel studio.

1958—The Blue House is opened to the public as the Museo Frida Kahlo.

GLOSSARY

Balero: Cup-and-ball toy

Cachuchas: Name of the group at the *Escuela Nacional Preparatoria* that wore crocheted, red-peaked caps.

Carcajadas: Belly laugh

Cinco: Five

Coyoacán: A town south of Mexico City where Frida was born.

De: Of

¡Extra!: Extra, a special edition of a newspaper.

Fisita: Diego's nickname for Frida

Frieda: German for "peace." Frida removed the "e" from her name when Hitler came to power.

Gangrene: The death and decay of body tissue caused by poor circulation.

Gringolandia: Frida's name for the United States

Herr: German for "Sir"

Huipil: Blouse

Internationale, The: Socialist song

¡La bailarina!: The ballerina!

La Malagueña: A popular mexican song often played by mariachi bands; its English translation is "The Woman from Málaga."

La prepa: Short for *Escuela Nacional Preparatoria*, National Preparatory School

Lieber: German for "dear guy." *Liebe* would be the term for a girl.

Mamá: Mother

Mariachi: A musician who plays Mexican songs

Mexicana, a la: The Mexican way, with courage

Mi jefe: My Chief

Mole: A spicy sauce of Mexican origin

No me olvides, amor mío: Don't forget me, my love

Oaxaca: A city in southeast Mexico

Panzón: Fatso

Peso: Mexican currency

Petates: Woven straw mats

Polio: Poliomyelitis, an infectious viral disease that causes paralysis and deformities.

Pulque: Fermented drink made from maguey-plant sap

Rebozo: Shawl

Sí: Yes

Tehuana: A native tribe of Mexico

Tehuantepec, Isthmus of: A narrow piece of land in southern Mexico

¡Viva la vida!: Long live life!

SOURCES

BOOKS

Dexter, Emma and Tanya Barson. *Frida Kahlo*. London: Tate Publishing, 2005.
Garza, Hedda. *Frida Kahlo*. New York: Chelsea House Publishers, 1994.
Grimberg, Salomon. *Frida Kahlo. North Dighton, Mass.: JG Press, 1997*. **Grimberg, Salomon**. I Will Never Forget You: Frida Kahlo to Niklaus Muray, Unpublished Photographs and Letters. *London: Tate Publishing, 2005.* **Herrera, Hayden**. Frida: A Biography of Frida Kahlo. *New York: Perennial, 2002.* **Kahlo, Isolda**. Frida Intima: Frida Kahlo (1907-1954). *Bogotá: Ediciones Dipon, 2004.* **Lowe, Sarah M.** The Diary of Frida Kahlo. *New York: Harry N. Abrams, Inc., 1995.* **Tibol, Raquel**. An Open Life: Frida Kahlo. *Albuquerque: University of New Mexico Press, 1993.* **Rivera, Diego**. My Art, My Life: An Autobiography. *New York: Dover Publications, Inc., 1991.* **Rivera, Guadalupe and Marie-Pierre Colle**. Frida's Fiestas: Recipes and Reminiscences of Life with Frida Kahlo. *New York: Clarkson Potter Publishers, 1994.* **Zamora, Martha**. Frida Kahlo: The Brush of Anguish. *San Francisco: Chronicle Books, 1990.* **Zamora, Martha**, *compiler.* The Letters of Frida Kahlo. *San Francisco: Chronicle Books, 1995.*

MOVIES AND DOCUMENTARIES

Frida: Naturaleza Viva. Director Paul Leduc. Radco, DVD 2003.
The Life and Times of Frida Kahlo. Director Amy Stechler Burns. PBS Paramount, DVD 2006.
Frida. Director Julic Taymor. Miramax Home Entertainment, DVD 2003.

WEB SITES

Answers.com. "Frida Kahlo." www.answers.com/topic/frida-kahlo
Artchive.com. "Frida Kahlo." www.artchive.com/k/kahlo.html
Artcyclopedia. "Frida Kahlo." www.artcyclopedia.com/artists/kahlo_frida.html
Brown, Amy. "Frida Kahlo: An Amazing Woman."
     www.amybrown.nct/women/frida.html
Falini, Daniela. "Frida Kahlo and Contemporary Thoughts." www.fridakahlo.it
Frida Kahlo.com. www.fridakahlo.com
González, Mike. "Frida Kahlo: A Life," June 2005.
     www.socialistreview.org.uk/article.php?articlenumber=9436
Kahlo, Frida. "Frida by Kahlo." www.fbuch.com/fridaby.htm
Laurier, Joanne. "What Made Frida Kahlo Remarkable?" 7 November 2002.
     www.wsws.org/articles/2002/nov2002/kahl-n07.shtml
Tripp, Adrienne. "Frida Kahlo: Life Portrait."
     www.planetsalsa.com/quepasa/frida_kahlo_self_portrait.htm
Tuchman, Phyllis. "Frida Kahlo" November 2002.
     www.smithsonianmag.com/issues/2002/november/frida.php

NOTES

Wilhelm (Guillermo) Kahlo
Frieda, lieber, Frieda: Herrera, *Frida*, p. 18.
Matilde Calderón de Kahlo
Mi jefe: Herrera, *Frida*, p. 14.
Chubby midget: Lowe, *The Diary of Frida Kahlo*, p. 282.
"Oh, *mamá:*" Tibol, *Frida Kahlo*, p. 38-39.
The *Cachuchas*
City of the World: Herrera, *Frida*, p. 116.
Diego
"Watch out, Diego!": Rivera, *My Art, My Life*, p. 75.
The Accident
"¡La bailarina!": Herrera, *Frida*, p. 49.
Life Begins Tomorrow
"I'm still alive": Tibol, *Frida Kahlo*, p. 44.
Recipe for Self-Portrait
Black hair silk girl: Lowe, *The Diary of Frida Kahlo*, p. 203.
Green: Ibid., p. 211.
"You Have Talent"
"Diego, come down!": Herrera, *Frida*, p. 87.
"Look, I have not": Ibid.
"I am very interested": Ibid.
"You have talent!": Ibid.
San Francisco
I belong to my owner: Herrera, *Frida*, p. 471.
Mother and Child
Dark-skinned: Lowe, *The Diary of Frida Kahlo*, p. 280.
"Look, Diego!": Herrera, *Frida*, p. 141.
Manhattan
It is terrifying: Garza, *Frida Kahlo*, p. 60.
Double Disgrace
She was my sister: Zamora, *The Letters of Frida Kahlo*, p. 61.
It is all about him: Lowe, *The Diary of Frida Kahlo*, p. 229.
It is going to take me years: Zamora, *The Letters of Frida Kahlo*, p. 61.
I suffered two grave accidents: Herrera, *Frida*, p. 107.
My Diego My Child
Why do I call him: Lowe, *The Diary of Frida Kahlo*, p. 235.
Diego my child: Ibid.
Self-Portrait with Cropped Hair
Men are kings: Herrera, *Frida*, p. 250.
Headlines
I don't know what they see: Herrera, *Frida*, p. 225.
not capable of painting: Ibid., p. xiii.

For that price: Ibid. p. 225.

Second Marriage

"Give your Cupid": Herrera, *Frida,*, p. 365.

"What Do I Live For?"

"What do I live for?": Herrera, *Frida*, p. 378.

"So that I live": Ibid., p. 379.

Nothing is equal: Lowe, *The Diary of Frida Kahlo*, p. 213.

"My darling child": Herrera, *Frida*, p. 422.

"*Chi*": Ibid.

My Diego: Lowe, *The Diary of Frida Kahlo*, p. 260.

Wounded Deer

I am not sick: Herrera, *Frida*, p. 410.

Lola's Gallery

"No artist in Mexico": Herrera, *Frida*, p. 361.

"Is she coming?": Paraphrase, Ibid., p. 406.

"Thanks to myself": Paraphrase, Ibid., p. 421.

Wings to Fly

There is only one: Lowe, *The Diary of Frida Kahlo*, p. 276.

You are killing yourself!: Ibid., p. 273.

I drink to drown my pain: Paraphrase, Zamora, *The Letters of Frida Kahlo*, p. 84.

Sleep: Lowe, *The Diary of Frida Kahlo*, p. 250.

Feet, what do I need them for: Ibid., p. 274.

¡Viva la vida! Long Live Life!

I hope the exit is joyful: Lowe, *The Diary of Frida Kahlo*, p. 285.

"I was shattered": Ibid., p. 270.

"I feel I am going to leave you": Rivera, *My Art, My Life*, p. 178.

"No me olvides"

No me olvides: Bernier-Grand, visit to the Blue House, Coyoacán, Mexico.

"Too late now I realized": Rivera, *My Art, My Life*, p. 180.

Life goes by: Lowe, *The Diary of Frida Kahlo*, p. 248.

Frida Kahlo: 1907-1954 and Beyond

"Please, don't forget me!": Zamora, *The Letters of Frida Kahlo*, p. 131.

Acknowledgments

The photographs and paintings in this book are used by permission and through the courtesy of:
Jacket *Self-portrait with Monkey* (1938), oil on Masonite overall: 16" x 12" (40.64 x 30.48 cm.), Albright-Knox Art Gallery, Buffalo, New York. Bequest of A. Conger Goodyear, 1966, © 2007 Banco de Mexico Diego Rivera & Frida Kahlo Museums Trust, Av. Cinco de mayo No. 2 Col. Centro, Del. Cuauhtemoc 06059, Mexico, D.F., Pg. 4 "Color Photo with Floral Background," photo by Nickolas Muray; © Nickolas Muray, Photo Archives/George Eastman Hous, Pg. 9 *My Grandparents, My Parents, and I* (1936), Digital Image©The Museum of Modern Art/Licensed by SCALA/Art Resource, NY©2007 Banco de Mexico Diego Rivera & Frida Kahlo Museums Trust, Av. Cinco de mayo No. 2 Col. Central, Del. Cuauhtemoc 06059, Mexico, D.F., Pg. 11 *Frida at 19* (1926), Museo Dolores Olmedo Patiño © 2007 Banco de Mexico Diego Rivera & Frida Kahlo Museums Trust, Av. Cinco de mayo No. 2 Col. Centro, Del. Cuauhtemoc 06059, Mexico, D.F., Pg. 12 *Portrait of Diego Rivera* (1937), The Jacques and Natasha Gelman Collection of Modern and Contemporary Mexican Art; courtesy of The Vergel Foundation; Fundación Cultural Parque Morelos (Muros); Costco and Comercial Mexicana. © 2007 Banco de Mexico Diego Rivera & Frida Kahlo Museums Trust, Av. Cinco de mayo No. 2 Col. Centro, Del. Cuauhtemoc 06059, Mexico, D.F., Pg. 15 *The Bus* (1929), Schalkwijk/Art Resource, NY © 2007 Banco de Mexico Diego Rivera & Frida Kahlo Museums Trust, Av. Cinco de mayo No. 2 Col. Centro, Del. Cuauhtemoc 06059, Mexico, D.F. , Pg. 20 *Portrait of Alicia Galant* (1927), Schalkwijk/Art Resource, NY © 2007 Banco de Mexico Diego Rivera & Frida Kahlo Museums Trust, Av. Cinco de mayo No. 2 Col. Centro, Del. Cuauhtemoc 06059, Mexico, D.F., Pg. 21 Detail from *Insurrection* (1928), Schalkwijk/Art Resource, NY © 2007 Banco de Mexico Diego Rivera & Frida Kahlo Museums Trust, Av. Cinco de mayo No. 2 Col. Centro, Del. Cuauhtemoc 06059, Mexico, D.F., Pg. 22 *Frida and Diego Rivera* (1930-1931), San Franciso Museum of Modern Art, Albert M., Bender Collection © 2007 Banco de Mexico Diego Rivera & Frida Kahlo Museums Trust, Av. Cinco de mayo No. 2 Col. Centro, Del. Cuauhtemoc 06059, Mexico, D.F., Pg. 24 *Self-portrait on the Border between Mexico and the United States* (1932) copyright©2007 Christie's Images Ltd. All rights reserved.©2007 Banco de Mexico Diego Rivera & Frida Kahlo Museums Trust, Av. Cinco de mayo No. 2 Col. Centro, Del. Cuauhtemoc 06059, Mexico, D.F., Pg. 29 *My Dress Hangs There* (1933), copyright©2007 Christie's Images Ltd. All rights reserved.©2007 Banco de Mexico Diego Rivera & Frida Kahlo Museums Trust, Av. Cinco de mayo No. 2 Col. Centro, Del. Cuauhtemoc 06059, Mexico, D.F., Pg. 30 *Portrait of Cristina Kahlo* (1928), "privately owned"©2007, Banco de Mexico Diego Rivera & Frida Kahlo Museums Trust, Av. Cinco de mayo No. 2 Col. Centro, Del. Cuauhtemoc 06059, Mexico, D.F., Pg. 33 *The Two Fridas* (1939), Schalkwijk/Art Resource, NY © 2007 Banco de Mexico Diego Rivera & Frida Kahlo Museums Trust, Av. Cinco de mayo No. 2 Col. Centro, Del. Cuauhtemoc 06059, Mexico, D.F., Pg. 35 *The Love Embrace, the Earth (Mexico), Diego, Me, and Senor Xolotl* (1949), The Jacques and Natasha Gelman Collection of Modern and Contemporary Mexican Art; courtesy of The Vergel Foundation; Fundación Cultural Parque Morelos (Muros); Costco and Comercial Mexicana. © 2007 Banco de Mexico Diego Rivera & Frida Kahlo Museums Trust, Av. Cinco de mayo No. 2 Col. Centro, Del. Cuauhtemoc 06059, Mexico, D.F., Pg. 37 *Self-portrait with Cropped Hair* (1940), Digital Image©The Museum of Modern Art/Licensed by SCALA/Art Resource, NY©2007 Banco de Mexico Diego Rivera & Frida Kahlo Museums Trust, Av. Cinco de mayo No. 2 Col. Central, Del. Cuauhtemoc 06059, Mexico, D.F., Pg. 39 *The Frame* (1938), CNAC/MNAM/Dist Reunion des Musées Nationaux/Art Resource, NY/ Banco de Mexico Diego Rivera & Frida Kahlo Museums Trust, Av. Cinco de mayo No. 2 Col. Centro, Del. Cuauhtemoc 06059, Mexico, D.F., Pg. 43 *Tree of Hope, Stand Firm* (1946), Isidore Ducasse Fine Arts/©2007 Banco de Mexico Diego Rivera & Frida Kahlo Museums Trust, Av. Cinco de mayo No. 2 Col. Centro, Del. Cuauhtemoc 06059, Mexico, D.F., Pg. 45 *The Little Deer* (1946), "La Venadita (The Little Deer)," collection of Dr. Carolyn Farb/ © 2007 Banco de Mexico Diego Rivera & Frida Kahlo Museums Trust, Av. Cinco de mayo No. 2 Col. Centro, Del. Cuauhtemoc 06059, Mexico, D.F., Pg. 48 *Self-Portrait as a Tehuana (Diego in My Thoughts)* (1948), *Portrait of Natasha Gelman* (1943), The Jacques and Natasha Gelman Collection of Modern and Contemporary Mexican Art; courtesy of The Vergel Foundation; Fundación Cultural Parque Morelos (Muros); Costco and Comercial Mexicana. © 2007 Banco de Mexico Diego Rivera & Frida Kahlo Museums Trust, Av. Cinco de mayo No. 2 Col. Centro, Del. Cuauhtemoc 06059, Mexico, D.F., Pg. 49 *Self-Portrait (dedicated to Leon Trotsky)* (1937): Oil on masonite, 30" x 24", National Museum of Women in the Arts, Washington, D.C. Gift of Honorable Clare Booth Luce/©2007 Banco de Mexico Diego Rivera & Frida Kahlo Museums Trust, Av. Cinco de mayo No. 2 Col. Centro, Del. Cuauhtemoc 06059, Mexico, D.F. , *The Chick* (1945), Schalkwijk/Art Resource, NY/© 2007 Banco de Mexico Diego Rivera & Frida Kahlo Museums Trust, Av. Cinco de mayo No. 2 Col. Centro, Del. Cuauhtemoc 06059, Mexico, D.F. , Pg. 51 *Without Hope* (1945), Schalkwijk/Art Resource, NY/© 2007 Banco de Mexico Diego Rivera & Frida Kahlo Museums Trust, Av. Cinco de mayo No. 2 Col. Centro, Del. Cuauhtemoc 06059, Mexico, D.F.
Pg. 52 *Viva la vida* (1954), Private Collection/Bridgeman Art Library/© 2007 Banco de Mexico Diego Rivera & Frida Kahlo Museums Trust, Av. Cinco de mayo No. 2 Col. Centro, Del. Cuauhtemoc 06059, Mexico, D.F.